Home for
Chinese New Year

This book is edited and designed by the Editorial Committee of *Cultural China* series

Story by Wei Jie
Illustration by Xu Can
Translation by Yijin Wert
Design by Su Liangliang

Copy Editor: Anna Nguyen
Editor: Wu Yuezhou
Editorial Director: Zhang Yicong

Senior Consultants: Sun Yong, Wu Ying, Yang Xinci
Managing Director and Publisher: Wang Youbu

ISBN: 978-1-60220-999-2

Address any comments about *Home for Chinese New Year* to:

Better Link Press
99 Park Ave
New York, NY 10016
USA

or

Shanghai Press and Publishing Development Company, Ltd.
F 7 Donghu Road, Shanghai, China (200031)
Email: comments_betterlinkpress@hotmail.com

Printed in China by Shenzhen Donnelley Printing Co., Ltd.

1 3 5 7 9 10 8 6 4 2

Home for Chinese New Year

A Story Told in English and Chinese

By Wei Jie and Xu Can

Translated by Yijin Wert

回家

Better Link Press

Jiajun called his father, "Daddy! It's almost Chinese New Year! When will you be home? I miss you very much."

Early next morning, Jiajun's father went to the train station to get his ticket. There was a long line by the ticket office. Everyone was trying to get home for the Chinese New Year.

家俊给爸爸打电话："爸爸，快过年啦，你什么时候到家呢？我很想你。"

第二天一早，家俊的爸爸去买火车票。售票处门前排着长长的队伍。大家都想回家过年呢。

After he bought his ticket, the excitement of being home in a few days kept him motivated as he worked on the construction site.

买好火车票，想着就可以回家了，家俊的爸爸在工地上好像有使不完的劲。

Finally it was time to travel. The day before New Year's Eve, the train station was packed with people eager to get home.

Jiajun's father couldn't help thinking of his son, while noticing in the crowd some children who looked to be around the same age as Jiajun, "Could he be as tall as these boys?"

终于到了回家的日子。小年夜，车站里挤满了想回家的人。

看着人群中和家俊差不多大小的孩子，家俊的爸爸忍不住想，"家俊也有这么高了吧？"

Travelers rushed to get on the train at the station.

火车就停在那里，可大家还是忍不住小跑着上车。

Jiajun's father was ready to relax once he found his seat. He wanted to eat an apple, but he couldn't find it in his bag.

He reached inside his coat pocket, and then pulled his hand out with relief.

家俊的爸爸在火车上坐定。吃个苹果吧。可是准备好的苹果找不到了。

他把手伸进大衣口袋里摸摸，又放心地把手拿了出来。

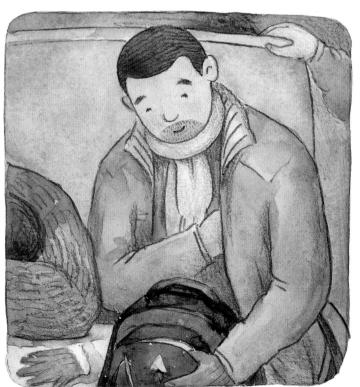

"Daddy, did you cross the Yangtze River yet?"

"爸爸，你过长江了吗？"

The train stopped temporarily. Jiajun's father checked his cell phone frequently to make sure he wouldn't miss a call from his son. He was waiting anxiously for the train to move again.

火车临时停车，家俊的爸爸隔一会儿就看手机，担心错过家俊的电话，又盼着火车尽快启动。

It was already midnight when Jiajun's father got off the train. He went into the waiting room of the long-distance bus station in order to get on the first bus in the next early morning.

下了火车已是半夜。家俊的爸爸来到长途汽车候车室，等天亮坐头班长途汽车。

The morning finally came. Jiajun's father got on the first bus.

天终于亮了。家俊的爸爸坐上了头班长途汽车。

Jiajun's father wanted to drink water, but he could not find his water bottle.

He reached inside his coat pocket, and then pulled his hand out with relief.

这时，家俊的爸爸想喝水，可是怎么也找不到那瓶水。

他把手伸进大衣口袋里摸摸，又放心地把手拿了出来。

"Daddy, Grandma has made you chicken soup. Grandpa said you would arrive at noon."

"爸爸，奶奶熬了鸡汤，爷爷说你中午就能到家。"

After getting off the bus, Jiajun's father got on a three-wheeled motorcycle.

下了长途汽车，家俊的爸爸又坐上了三轮摩托车。

Through the window, Jiajun's father saw the snowflakes. Jiajun loved snow very much! Whatever he liked, his father liked, too. However, Jiajun's father hoped it would stop snowing very soon as he wanted to be home for the New Year's Eve.

车窗外飘起了雪花。家俊最喜欢下雪了！家俊喜欢的，爸爸也喜欢。可现在，家俊的爸爸希望雪能停下来，要赶回家过年呢。

It was about dusk when he got off the three-wheeled motorcycle. Then he got on a ferry boat.

下了三轮摩托车，已经是傍晚，家俊的爸爸乘上了渡船。

It was getting very cold. Jiajun's father wanted to put his gloves on, but he could not find his gloves.

He reached inside his coat pocket again, and then pulled his hand out with relief.

天太冷了，家俊的爸爸想戴上手套，可是手套又找不着了。

他把手伸进大衣口袋里摸摸，又放心地把手拿了出来。

"Daddy, where are you? Mom and I have been waiting for you on the street."

"爸爸，你现在到哪里了？妈妈和我一直在路口等。"

After he got off the ferry boat, the snow became
heavy, and it started to get dark.

下了渡船，雪更大了，天有点黑了……

"Daddy, Mom asked you to stay at my aunt's house tonight. The weather forecast calls for less snow tomorrow. See you tomorrow!"

"爸爸，妈妈让你到二姨家住一夜。天气预报说明天雪就小了，明天见。"

Jiajun's father felt warm and energetic after having a bowl of noodle soup at a local restaurant. "Today is New Year's Eve. It is the day for family reunions. I must be home," Jiajun's father thought.

家俊的爸爸在小饭馆里吃了碗面，全身都暖和了，力气也有了。"今天是除夕，是合家团圆的日子。一定要赶回家！"家俊的爸爸想。

The snow was up to his knees and it was very cold. Jiajun's father decided to trudge on. Suddenly, a gust of wind blew away his scarf.

He reached inside his coat pocket again, and then pulled his hand out with relief.

积雪深到膝盖，天很冷。家俊的爸爸决定走回家。突然，一阵风吹走了他的围巾。

他把手伸进大衣口袋里摸摸，又放心地把手拿了出来。

Bang! Bang! Bang! Jiajun's father could hear the firecrackers going off in the distance. He knew he was very close to his home, but he was so tired that he decided to take a break.

Then he saw a little puppy running towards him. It was Jiajun's little puppy Wangwang. He was coming to welcome Jiajun's father home.

噼里啪啦，远处隐约传来了鞭炮声。家应该不远了！可是，家俊爸爸实在太累了，便停下休息一会儿。

这时，他看见一条小狗朝他跑来。哦，是家俊的小狗旺旺，它来迎接家俊的爸爸回家。

Jiajun's father finally made it home.

终于到家了。

Jiajun's father reached into his coat pocket, and carefully pulled out a watch. Jiajun was thrilled to receive the gift from his father. He put it on his wrist immediately.

家俊的爸爸把手伸进大衣口袋里，小心翼翼地掏出一只手表。家俊接过爸爸的新年礼物，高兴地戴到手腕上。

Then Jiajun and his father went out to set off firecrackers together.

接着，家俊和爸爸一起出去放鞭炮。

It was time for the New Year's Eve dinner. The whole family sat around the table and had a lovely reunion feast.

该吃年夜饭了！一家人热热闹闹地围坐在圆桌边，吃起了丰盛的团圆饭。

During the holiday season, Jiajun's father was busy cleaning their house, putting up red couplets on their door and making snowmen with Jiajun. Jiajun was with his father every day.

正月里，爸爸每天都有事情做，洒扫庭院，贴对联，和家俊一起堆雪人。家俊天天黏着爸爸。

Jiajun enjoyed every moment with his father.

One day, while they were making the rabbit lantern for the Lantern Festival, Jiajun's father said, "I am leaving for work in the city tomorrow." Jiajun became sad as he knew it was time to say good-bye.

和爸爸在一起，家俊觉得开心极了。

一天，他们在一起做着元宵节的兔子灯，爸爸说："家俊啊，明天我得回城去工作了。"一想到要和爸爸暂时分别，家俊高兴不起来了。

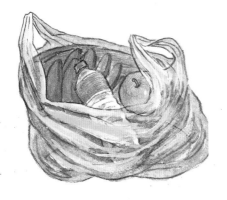

The next day, Jiajun handed his father a bag before he left, "Daddy, this is from me. Please don't lose it. I'm letting you use my green scarf," said Jiajun. His father took the bag with a smile.

第二天，爸爸出发前，家俊递给爸爸一个袋子，说："爸爸，这是我给你的，希望你不要弄丢了！我的绿围巾也让你用吧。"爸爸微笑着接过袋子。

Jiajun's father said goodbye to his family and
went on his journey back to the city …

与亲人一一道别后，爸爸又出发了……

It's a Chinese tradition for everyone to return home on New Year's Eve no matter where they are to reunite with family and enjoy a family reunion dinner.

在中国，每到春节，散落在不同地方的人会从四面八方回到自己的家，只为在除夕之夜全家团圆，和家人吃一顿团圆饭。

Chinese New Year 春节

It is the most important holiday in China. Although it is on the first day of the first month of the lunar calendar, the celebration usually lasts to the 15th day of the first month. During the celebration season, people have family reunion dinners, hand out lucky money bags, set off firecrackers, put up red couplets on doors, clean their houses and visit families and friends.

这是中国最重要的节日。虽定为农历正月初一，但从除夕开始一直延续到正月十五。期间有着各种节庆活动，比如合家团聚吃年夜饭、分发红包、放鞭炮、贴对联、洒扫除尘、互访拜年等等。

Lantern Festival 元宵节

It is on the 15th day of the first month of the lunar calendar. This is also the last day of the New Year celebration season. On that day, people usually eat *tangyuan* (rice dumplings) and enjoy beautiful lantern displays.

每年农历正月十五，也是春节节庆活动的最后一天。人们在这一天要吃汤圆，赏花灯。